FAMILIES

A Look at Life Around the World

By Joanna Brundle

KidHaven PUBLISHING

Published in 2019 by
KidHaven Publishing, an Imprint of Greenhaven Publishing, LLC
353 3rd Avenue
Suite 255
New York, NY 10010

Designer: Jasmine Pointer
Editor: Kirsty Holmes

Photocredits: Abbreviations: l-left, r-right, b-bottom, t-top, c-center, m-middle. All images are courtesy of Shutterstock.com. With thanks to Getty Images, Thinkstock Photo and iStockphoto. Front cover - CRS PHOTO, Monkey Business Images, Petrenko Andriy. 2 - Nolte Lourens. 4t - Monkey Business Images. 4b – CREATISTA. 5t - Gladskikh Tatiana. 5b - Blend Images. 6t - Tom Wang. 6m – rasika108. 7t - Rawpixel.com. 7b - Felix Mizioznikov. 8 - Jordi C. 9t - szefei. 9b - Monkey Business Images. 10t - Vixit. 10mr - hecke61. 10b - De Visu. 11t - Vladimir Kovalchuk. 11b - longtaildog. 12 - Natalia Kirichenko. 13 - Ms Jane Campbell. 14 - Orlok. 15 - Sk Hasan Ali. 16m - espies. 16r - Eastfenceimage. 17 - humphery. 18 - wong sze yuen. 19t - Monkey Business Images. 19b - Sharad Raval. 20 - OskarAanmoen. 21t - Lorna Roberts. 21b - dimakig. 22tl - Tory Kallman. 21r - Alexey Osokin.

Cataloging-in-Publication Data

Names: Brundle, Joanna.
Title: Families / Joanna Brundle.
Description: New York : KidHaven Publishing, 2019. | Series: A look at life around the world | Includes glossary and index.
Identifiers: ISBN 9781534528314 (pbk.) | ISBN 9781534528338 (library bound) | ISBN 9781534528321 (6 pack) | ISBN 9781534528345 (ebook)
Subjects: LCSH: Families--Juvenile literature.
Classification: LCC HQ744.B78 2019 | DDC 306.85--dc23

Printed in the United States of America

CPSIA compliance information: Batch #BW19KL: For further information contact Greenhaven Publishing LLC, New York, New York at 1-844-317-7404.

Please visit our website, www.greenhavenpublishing.com. For a free color catalog of all our high-quality books, call toll free 1-844-317-7404 or fax 1-844-317-7405.

CONTENTS

Page 4 What Is a Family?

Page 6 Small and Large Families

Page 8 Extended Families

Page 10 Nomadic Families

Page 12 Migrant Families

Page 14 Refugee Families

Page 16 Grandparents

Page 18 Family Life

Page 20 Royal Families

Page 22 Animal Families

Page 23 Glossary

Page 24 Index

Words that look like this can be found in the glossary on page 23.

WHAT IS A FAMILY?

All around the world, children just like you live in all sorts of families. Some live with both their parents, but some live with just their mommy or just their daddy. Some have two daddies or two mommies. Some live with grandparents or stepparents. Some are adopted or live with foster families or with their older siblings.

This large family has gathered together to celebrate a birthday.

In this book, we will travel around the world, looking at many families living very different lives. As you read, think about how the families are similar to or different from your family. Whatever sort of family you live in, your family is made up of the people who love and care for you.

SMALL AND LARGE FAMILIES

In 1979, the government in China passed laws to say that parents were only allowed to have one child. Since 2016, two children have been allowed.

In some rural parts of Africa, Asia, and South America, families with as many as ten children are common.

The Radford family has 20 children: 9 girls and 11 boys. They are the largest family in the UK and one of the largest in the world.

This large family has gathered together for a photograph. Do you have family photographs at home?

Many very large families have sets of twins, triplets, or quadruplets. Benin, in central Africa, has more sets of twins than anywhere else in the world.

Twins often run in families.

EXTENDED FAMILIES

This family from Nigeria lives in a group of houses in the same village.

Large family groups are called extended families. In Asia and Africa, it is common for three or four generations of the same family to live together. Uncles, aunts, nephews, and nieces may also live in the same home or in groups of houses nearby, called a compound.

In traditional Indian families, the eldest son takes his wife to live with his parents. She is expected to look after the family. Several generations living together is less common in the United States and the United Kingdom.

Some children are cared for by their grandparents.

Children may spend their days at a nursery instead of being at home.

NOMADIC FAMILIES

Families that travel from place to place are called nomadic families. Bedouin families in North Africa travel around looking for water and grazing for their goats and camels.

In Mongolia, whole families live together in tents called yurts. Yurts can be moved easily when the families move on to find fresh grazing for their animals.

A Mongolian Family in Their Yurt

The Nenets people of northern Russia are reindeer <u>herders</u>. The reindeer provide meat and skins that are used to make tents and clothing. Each year, Nenets families move with their herd from summer to winter pastures. They travel on sleds pulled by the reindeer.

Nenets families live together in a tent called a chum.

MIGRANT FAMILIES

Many families migrate to Australia to enjoy the outdoor lifestyle.

Some families choose to move to a different country in search of a better life. These families are called migrant families. Much of the population of the United States is made up of families who originally came from other countries. These include Italy, Ireland, and Mexico.

Many families have migrated from eastern European countries like Poland and Latvia to western European countries like Germany. The parents of these families have come to look for work. Children in migrant families learn a new language and about the values and culture of their new home.

The Children's Parade, Notting Hill Carnival, London

These children's grandparents migrated from the Caribbean in the 1950s and 1960s.

REFUGEE FAMILIES

These children are refugees from a war in Syria.

Refugee families are families that have been forced to leave their homes to escape from danger. They travel to other countries to find safety from war or starvation. Some have been mistreated in their home countries. Some refugee families live in tents in refugee camps. Often, they long to return home.

The Rohingya are a group of people who have lived in Myanmar for generations. The government says they have no right to be there. Thousands of families have been forced to leave. They have had to walk very long distances.

This Rohingya family is escaping to Bangladesh.

GRANDPARENTS

Do you have grandparents?
Do they look after you sometimes?

In Kazakhstan, there is a custom that eldest sons should be brought up by grandparents. In China, it is common for children to live with their grandparents, leaving the parents free to work wherever they can.

In some countries, elder family members are greatly respected for their wisdom. In the Philippines, for example, children greet their grandparents by kneeling before them. In India, grandparents are the heads of the family. They give advice and have the final say on any disagreements.

In Korea and China, younger family members are expected to care for the elderly.

FAMILY LIFE

All around the world, families enjoy being together and having fun. In snowy countries like Sweden and Switzerland, families enjoy skiing and snowboarding together. Families in Australia enjoy spending time at the beach or having a barbecue. In the United States, family visits to baseball games are popular.

How does your family like to spend time together?

Eating together is an important part of family life all over the world. In Mediterranean countries like Spain and Italy, families love to gather together to eat outside. Lunch can last all afternoon!

What are your favorite family meals?

In Japan, traditional families like to sit together on the floor to eat. In parts of Asia, it is common for families to cook and eat outside their houses.

ROYAL FAMILIES

The Royal Family of Norway

A royal family is made up of a monarch and his or her extended family. Countries with a royal family are called monarchies. A total of 43 countries have a royal family. They include Thailand, Spain, Denmark, Bahrain, Japan, and Belgium.

When a monarch dies or abdicates, another member of the family takes their place. This is usually the eldest son or daughter of the monarch. Members of a royal family work together to support the monarch in carrying out his or her duties.

The Royal Family of the United Kingdom

Emperor Akihito and the Imperial Family of Japan

A Japanese emperor is always followed by a prince, never a princess.

ANIMAL FAMILIES

Orca offspring may live with their parents all their lives.

Lions nuzzle and rub heads to strengthen family bonds.

Like us, some animals live with other family members. Elephants, lions, chimpanzees, wolves, and orcas all live in close family groups. Elephant calves live in herds with their mothers and aunts. Wolf cubs are brought up by both parents.

GLOSSARY

abdicates	decides to give up being monarch, often due to old age or ill health
adopted	legally looked after, on a permanent basis, by parents not related to the child
foster families	families that look after children, usually for a short time, who are not related to the children
generations	groups of people from the same family or society who are roughly the same age
government	group of people who have the authority to run a country and decide its laws
grazing	land where animals feed on grass and other vegetation
herders	people who make their living breeding and caring for groups of animals
monarch	a ruler, such as a king or a queen
population	a group of people or the number of people living in a certain place
siblings	brothers or sisters
starvation	suffering or death caused by lack of food
stepparents	parents who are married to the mother or father of a child but are not that child's own father or mother

INDEX

Africa 6–8, 10

animals 10, 22

Asia 6, 8–11, 14–17, 19–21

aunt 8, 22

Australia 12, 18

eating 19

Europe 7, 9, 12–14, 18–21

generations 8–9, 15

grandparents 9, 13, 16–17

houses 8, 19

parents 4, 6, 9, 13, 16, 22

-daddy 4

-mommy 4

South America 6

travel 5, 10–11, 14–15

uncles 8

United Kingdom 7, 9, 12–13

United States 9, 12, 18